QUANTUM HEARTS

Aria Nova

GLOBAL
PUBLISHING
SOLUTIONS

QUANTUM HEARTS by Aria Nova

Published by Global Publishing Solutions, LLC
923 Fieldside Drive
Matteson, Illinois 60443
www.globalpublishingsolutions.com

This book or parts thereof may not be reproduced in any form, stored in a retrieval system, or transmitted in any form by any means—electronic, mechanical, photocopy, recording, or otherwise—without prior permission of the publisher, except as provided by United States of America copyright law.

Copyright © 2024 by Aria Nova

All rights reserved.

International Standard Book Number:
9798330294220
E-book International Standard Book Number:
9798330294237

Unless otherwise indicated, all the names, characters, businesses, places, events, and incidents in this book are either the product of the author's imagination or used in a fictitious manner. Any resemblance to actual persons, living or dead, or actual events is purely coincidental.

Printed in the United States of America

TABLE OF CONTENTS

Prologue: A Love Across Dimensions i
The Enigmatic Amulet 1
The Quantum Connection 5
The Journey to the Heart 9
Across the Ages 13
The Moonlit Meadow 17
Love Against the Odds 21
The Quantum Dilemma 26
Unraveling the Mystery 30
The Infinite Possibilities 34
Convergence 38
Epilogue: Love Beyond Dimensions 43

PROLOGUE: A LOVE ACROSS DIMENSIONS

In the quiet corridors of existence, where the boundaries of time and space blur, a love story unfolds that defies the laws of the known universe. Emily, a brilliant astrophysicist with an insatiable curiosity for the cosmos, stumbles upon an artifact that transcends the limits of human understanding—an ancient amulet pulsating with an otherworldly energy.

Unbeknownst to Emily, this artifact is a key to unlocking a connection that spans across dimensions, reaching into the fabric of time itself. As she investigates the mysterious amulet, she unwittingly becomes entangled in a love story that defies the ordinary constraints of life.

On the other side of this cosmic tether stands David, a physicist equally enthralled by the mysteries of the universe. Drawn together by forces beyond their comprehension, Emily and David discover a form of communication that transcends the physical realm. Letters, seemingly propelled by the very essence of quantum entanglement, traverse the ages, carrying with them the emotions, thoughts, and dreams of two souls connected across time.

Their love is a dance of particles in the vast expanse of the quantum realm—a dance that defies the conventional, challenges the scientific mind, and tugs at the heartstrings of those who witness its unfolding. But as they navigate the uncharted territories of their extraordinary connection, they must confront the ethical dilemmas, scientific implications, and societal skepticism that accompany such a phenomenon.

"Quantum Hearts" is a tale of love, not bound by the ticking of the clock or the ticking of the heart, but by the very essence of existence. As Emily and David venture into the unexplored territories of their quantum connection, the universe holds its breath, witnessing a love story written in the language of the cosmos—a story that spans the ages and reaches beyond the boundaries of time and space.

Emily Harper had always been drawn to the mysteries of the cosmos. The night sky, studded with twinkling stars, held secrets that whispered to her curious mind. As an astrophysicist, her days were spent deciphering the language of the universe, but it was a chance encounter with an ancient artifact that would lead her into the uncharted territories of a love that transcended the bounds of time.

It was a rainy Tuesday evening when Emily found herself at the dusty entrance of an antiquities shop nestled between modern buildings. The air inside was thick with the scent of aged books and the distant memories of forgotten eras. Wandering through the narrow aisles, Emily's eyes fell upon a display case, its glass surfaces clouded with the passage of time.

Within the case lay the centerpiece of the shop—a small amulet, its delicate chain intertwined with the threads of destiny. The amulet itself seemed unremarkable at first glance, but as Emily's fingers traced its intricate patterns, a subtle hum resonated in the air. It was a vibration that seemed to reverberate through her very being, as if the amulet held a secret energy waiting to be unleashed.

Intrigued, Emily inquired about the origins of the mysterious artifact. The shopkeeper, an elderly man with a twinkle in his eye, spoke of legends surrounding the amulet—a tale of a love so profound that it defied the boundaries of time. The amulet, he explained, was said to be a conduit for a connection that could transcend the ages, linking two souls across the vast expanse of the universe.

Enthralled by the romantic notion, Emily hesitated only briefly before deciding to make the amulet her own. Little did she know that this seemingly innocuous choice would set into motion a series of events that would unravel the very fabric of reality.

As Emily left the shop that evening, the amulet nestled against her chest, she felt a strange warmth spreading through her. Unbeknownst to her, on the other side of existence, in a realm not bound by the ticking of clocks or the limitations of physical presence, David, a physicist with a penchant for the extraordinary, would soon become entangled in the same cosmic web.

The stage was set, the amulet pulsating with latent energy, and the universe holding its breath as Emily and David's destinies converged around the enigmatic amulet—a key to a love that would bridge the gaps between stars and span the ages. Little did they know, the journey they were about to embark upon would transcend the known boundaries of human experience, setting the stage for a love story written in the quantum language of the cosmos.

THE ENIGMATIC AMULET

Emily Harper had always been drawn to the mysteries of the cosmos. The night sky, studded with twinkling stars, held secrets that whispered to her curious mind. As an astrophysicist, her days were spent deciphering the language of the universe, but it was a chance encounter with an ancient artifact that would lead her into the uncharted territories of a love that transcended the bounds of time.

It was a rainy Tuesday evening when Emily found herself at the dusty entrance of an antiquities shop nestled between modern buildings. The air inside was thick with the scent of aged books and the distant memories of forgotten eras. Wandering through the narrow aisles, Emily's eyes fell upon a display case, its glass surfaces clouded with the passage of time.

Within the case lay the centerpiece of the shop—a small amulet, its delicate chain intertwined with the threads of destiny. The amulet itself seemed unremarkable at first glance, but as Emily's fingers traced its intricate patterns, a subtle hum resonated in the air. It was a vibration that seemed to reverberate through her very being, as if the amulet held a secret energy waiting to be unleashed.

Intrigued, Emily inquired about the origins of the mysterious artifact. The shopkeeper, an elderly man with a twinkle in his eye, spoke of legends surrounding the amulet—a tale of a love so profound that it defied the boundaries of time. The amulet, he explained, was said to be a conduit for a connection that could transcend the ages, linking two souls across the vast expanse of the universe.

Enthralled by the romantic notion, Emily hesitated only briefly before deciding to make the amulet her own. Little did she know that this seemingly innocuous choice would set into motion a series of events that would unravel the very fabric of reality.

As Emily left the shop that evening, the amulet nestled against her chest, she felt a strange warmth spreading through her. Unbeknownst to her, on the other side of existence, in a realm not bound by the ticking of clocks or the limitations of physical presence, David, a physicist with a penchant for the extraordinary, would soon become entangled in the same cosmic web.

The stage was set, the amulet pulsating with latent energy, and the universe holding its breath as Emily and David's destinies converged around the enigmatic amulet—a key to a love that would bridge the gaps between stars and span the ages. Little did they know, the journey they were about to embark upon would transcend the known boundaries of human experience, setting the stage for a love story written in the quantum language of the cosmos.

THE QUANTUM CONNECTION

In the days that followed Emily's acquisition of the enigmatic amulet, an invisible thread wove itself through the tapestry of the universe, connecting her to a presence unbeknownst to her. As she delved into her daily routines, the amulet nestled against her skin seemed to hum with a frequency only she could feel.

One evening, as Emily sat in her dimly lit study, surrounded by the soft glow of her computer screens and the scent of well-worn books, an unexpected sensation enveloped her. It was as if the air itself was charged with a peculiar energy. A soft whisper echoed in the room, carrying words that seemed to materialize from the depths of the cosmos.

"Emily," the voice whispered, gentle and ethereal. It was a voice that transcended the barriers of sound, echoing through the corridors of her mind. Startled yet strangely comforted, Emily glanced around, half-expecting to find a presence in the room.

"Who's there?" she whispered into the stillness, the question lingering in the air like a shimmering constellation.

Across the expanse of existence, in a realm untouched by time, David experienced a similar phenomenon. The amulet he had obtained resonated with an energy that transcended the tangible. As he immersed himself in the equations and theories that defined his work, a subtle awareness began to unfurl within him—a connection to someone he had never met, yet whose presence echoed through the quantum realm.

"David," the whisper reached him, a voice that seemed to ride the wavelengths of the universe. It stirred something deep within him, a recognition that surpassed logic and reason.

In their respective spaces, Emily and David tentatively responded to the mysterious voices that seemed to traverse the boundaries of reality. They exchanged words—thoughts, dreams, fragments of their inner worlds—without uttering a single sound. The amulet, now a conduit for a quantum connection, facilitated a form of communication that transcended the limitations of spoken language.

As they navigated this uncharted territory, a profound understanding blossomed between them. Time became fluid, and the boundaries of space blurred as they exchanged fragments of their lives, thoughts dancing through the quantum ether.

In the quiet hours of the night, Emily and David found solace in this extraordinary connection. Unbeknownst to them, their thoughts and emotions wove a delicate tapestry, a shared consciousness that defied the conventional constraints of human interaction.

The quantum connection, initiated by the enigmatic amulet, became a bridge between two souls suspended in the vastness of the cosmos. Little did they realize that this silent conversation would evolve into a love story written in the language of quantum entanglement—a story that unfolded across dimensions, uniting two hearts in a dance that transcended the ordinary and embraced the extraordinary.

THE JOURNEY TO THE HEART

The days turned into weeks, and the quantum connection between Emily and David deepened. What began as an enigmatic encounter with an ancient amulet now evolved into a silent symphony of thoughts and emotions that echoed through the corridors of time.

Emily, sitting by the glow of her computer screen, felt an urge to share her world with David in a more tangible form. The quantum connection, while ethereal and enchanting, begged for a more grounded expression. Inspired by an old-world charm, she decided to put pen to paper, writing her thoughts and dreams in letters that transcended the boundaries of time.

In the quiet of her study, surrounded by the scent of ink and the soft rustling of paper, Emily began crafting a letter. The words flowed effortlessly as she narrated the stories of her days—the thrill of unraveling cosmic mysteries, the warmth of a morning coffee, and the quiet contemplation beneath a canvas of stars.

With each stroke of the pen, Emily felt a sense of connection that surpassed the digital whispers of the quantum realm. These letters, tangible and timeless, became vessels carrying the essence of her existence, intended to traverse the quantum expanse and reach David in a realm where the ticking of clocks held no dominion.

As Emily sealed the first letter with an antique wax seal, she couldn't shake the feeling that, in doing so, she was not just sending words but a piece of her soul across the cosmic currents.

On the other side of the quantum connection, David, too, felt the impulse to manifest his thoughts in a tangible form. Inspired by Emily's gesture, he embarked on the art of letter writing—a practice seemingly lost in the digital age. His words, carefully chosen and imbued with the spirit of a fellow explorer, flowed onto parchment.

In his letters, David spoke of the wonders of scientific discovery, the dance of particles, and the ceaseless pursuit of understanding the mysteries that bound the universe together. Each sentence carried the weight of his passion, a passion that reached across dimensions and beckoned Emily to join him in the exploration of the cosmos.

Through the exchange of these timeless letters, Emily and David discovered a connection that transcended the immediate and the ephemeral. The paper, once silent and still, now bore witness to a dance of words that spanned across ages—a dance that celebrated the beauty of human connection in a world where time was but a fleeting illusion.

The letters, suspended in the quantum currents, became a testament to a love story written in ink and sealed with the promise of a connection that would endure the test of time. As Emily and David continued to exchange their handwritten expressions, the cosmic dance of their intertwined destinies gained momentum, propelling them further into the unexplored realms of the heart and the quantum unknown.

ACROSS THE AGES

As the timeless letters traversed the quantum currents, a phenomenon unfolded—an exploration of shared experiences across the tapestry of time. Emily and David, separated by the constraints of their respective eras, found themselves navigating the echoes of each other's lives in a dance that transcended the ordinary boundaries of existence.

Emily's letters, carefully written on parchment and sealed with the warmth of her soul, became windows into her world. David, immersed in the ink-stained pages, felt the pulsating rhythm of her existence—the hum of her thoughts, the cadence of her laughter, and the quiet contemplation beneath the expansive canvas of stars.

In response, David's letters painted vivid landscapes of his reality—a world where scientific inquiry and the pursuit of knowledge were the guiding stars. Emily, reading his words, felt the pull of the cosmos, the yearning to understand the universe's intricate design through the lens of a kindred spirit.

As the letters crisscrossed through the quantum connection, a beautiful exchange unfolded. Emily, with the amulet clasped against her chest, felt the resonance of David's world—the rustle of parchment, the flicker of candlelight, and the profound silence of a physicist lost in contemplation. David, in turn, sensed the cosmic melodies of Emily's universe—the soft hum of telescopes, the scent of aged books, and the exhilaration of discovering new celestial wonders.

Their connection deepened as they explored the intricacies of their lives across the ages. Emily, through the ink-stained letters, walked through the cobbled streets of David's era, marveling at the advancements and challenges of a world on the brink of scientific revolution. David, in the ethereal dance of their connection, witnessed the blossoming of Emily's passion amidst the stars—a passion that echoed through the corridors of time.

As the quantum currents carried their shared experiences, Emily and David discovered a profound truth—the essence of their connection was not confined to a specific moment or era. Through the dance of letters, they transcended the limitations of time, forming a bridge that linked their souls in a perpetual exploration of the cosmic unknown.

The letters, suspended in the quantum realm, became artifacts of a love story that defied the linear progression of time. Through the ink and parchment, Emily and David etched their intertwined destinies onto the fabric of the universe—a story that unfolded but in a continuous, harmonious symphony across the ages.

And so, the dance persisted—a dance that celebrated the beauty of shared experiences, the resonance of kindred spirits, and the boundless nature of a connection that echoed through the corridors of time, uniting two hearts in a journey that transcended the boundaries of past, present, and future.

THE MOONLIT MEADOW

In the heart of the scientific enclave where David immersed himself in the pursuit of knowledge, the enigmatic amulet served as a silent witness to the unfolding mysteries of the cosmos. As the letters between Emily and David continued their timeless dance, a shared curiosity emerged—a yearning to understand the very fabric of the connection that bound them across the quantum expanse.

David, driven by both the passion for his work and the inexplicable pull of the quantum connection, dedicated himself to unraveling the scientific enigma at the core of their extraordinary communication.

The laboratory, adorned with instruments of precision and the hum of computers processing vast datasets, became the stage for David's quest. Guided by the whispers of the amulet and the echo of Emily's thoughts, he delved into the intricacies of quantum entanglement—

a phenomenon that challenged the very foundations of conventional science.

Through meticulous experiments and tireless exploration, David sought to comprehend the nature of their connection. The amulet, now a centerpiece in his scientific endeavors, pulsated with a rhythm that seemed to resonate with the underlying fabric of reality.

In the quiet moments of revelation, as David deciphered the intricacies of entangled particles and the principles governing the quantum realm, a realization dawned upon him. The amulet, a conduit for their connection, acted as a bridge not only between two hearts but also between the quantum and classical worlds.

In his laboratory notes, David recorded the patterns of their communication—the fluctuations in quantum states, the synchronicity of thoughts, and the emergence of a language that transcended the boundaries of conventional understanding. The letters, written across time and space, were not mere transmissions but intricately woven expressions encoded in the very essence of quantum entanglement.

With each revelation, the scientific community became intrigued by David's groundbreaking work. The enigmatic amulet, once a relic of romantic folklore, now held the potential to revolutionize the understanding of the quantum realm and the intricacies of interdimensional communication.

Yet, in the pursuit of scientific discovery, David grappled with a dichotomy. The very connection that fueled his groundbreaking research also posed ethical questions. Was it ethical to unravel the mysteries of a connection that seemed to transcend the boundaries of privacy and conventional understanding?

As David stood at the precipice of scientific revelation, he pondered the implications of his discoveries. The amulet, pulsating with the silent echoes of Emily's thoughts, became both a beacon guiding him through uncharted scientific territories and a mirror reflecting the ethical complexities of their shared journey.

The laboratory, once a sanctuary for scientific inquiry, now bore witness to a delicate dance between curiosity and conscience—a dance that would ultimately shape the destiny of the quantum connection and the love story that unfolded across the realms of science and the heart.

LOVE AGAINST THE ODDS

In the wake of David's groundbreaking scientific discoveries, the quantum connection between Emily and him reached a pivotal juncture. The allure of exploration, both scientific and emotional, propelled them into uncharted territories where the boundaries of love and the laws of physics intertwined.

As David's work gained acclaim within the scientific community, the world became aware of the enigmatic amulet and its role in facilitating an unprecedented connection. Speculations arose, debates ensued, and the very nature of their unique bond became a subject of fascination and skepticism.

Emily, an astrophysicist grounded in the tangible world of celestial bodies and cosmic forces, grappled with the implications of their connection being laid bare for public scrutiny. The warmth of the amulet against her skin now mingled with the heat of media attention and the relentless gaze of those who sought to dissect the intricacies of their love story.

The whispers of doubt echoed not only in the scientific community but also in the corridors of their own hearts. As the quantum connection became a topic of debate, the fabric of their love story faced the strain of external judgments and societal expectations.

Despite the challenges, Emily and David found solace in the unwavering bond they shared—a connection that transcended the cacophony of voices questioning the legitimacy of their love. They stood together against the odds; their hearts intertwined in a dance that defied the conventional norms of relationships.

In the face of public scrutiny, they became pioneers of a love that surpassed the constraints of societal expectations. Their journey, now intricately woven with threads of vulnerability and resilience, became a testament to the strength of a connection that thrived against the odds.

As the world observed their story unfold, Emily and David confronted not only the scientific complexities of their connection but also the emotional intricacies that defined their relationship. The amulet, once a silent witness, now bore the weight of public opinion, and its significance extended beyond the realm of quantum entanglement.

Through letters, conversations, and shared moments, Emily and David navigated the challenges of being at the center of a cosmic love story. The quantum connection, once a source of intimate communion, now faced the scrutiny of a world grappling with the unfamiliar.

Yet, in the face of adversity, Emily and David remained steadfast. Their love, forged in the crucible of cosmic connection and scientific curiosity, became a beacon—a symbol of resilience, authenticity, and the enduring power of a bond that transcended the boundaries of both time and societal norms.

Emily and David embraced the complexities of love against the odds. Their hearts, entwined by the threads of quantum entanglement, beat in harmony, echoing a melody that resonated through the quantum and emotional landscapes of their shared existence. The journey continued—a love story written in the quantum language of the cosmos, a story that defied the odds and embraced the extraordinary tapestry of their interconnected destinies.

THE QUANTUM DILEMMA

As the world marveled at the unprecedented love story unfolding between Emily and David, the quantum connection faced a crossroads—a dilemma that echoed through the corridors of their hearts and the scientific community alike.

The whispers of the amulet, once a symphony of shared thoughts and emotions, now carried a weight—a weight of ethical questions and the complexities of tampering with the delicate fabric of quantum entanglement.

In the hallowed halls of academia, David found himself standing at the forefront of a scientific revolution. The amulet, with its pulsating energy, had become a focal point of intrigue, curiosity, and, inevitably, controversy. The very essence of their connection, once a source of solace and wonder, now posed profound questions about the ethical implications of unraveling the mysteries of the quantum realm.

As the scientific community clamored for answers, David grappled with the quantum dilemma. The connection he shared with Emily, though extraordinary, sparked debates about the boundaries of privacy, the consequences of meddling with the quantum unknown, and the ethical responsibility inherent in pushing the limits of scientific inquiry.

Emily, too, felt the weight of the quantum dilemma pressing upon her. The letters, once a conduit for shared experiences, now bore witness to a world where the intimate details of their connection were laid bare for scrutiny. The very foundation of their love story faced the risk of being overshadowed by the ethical quandaries that emerged from their quantum entanglement.

In the quiet moments of reflection, Emily and David confronted the choices before them. The quantum dilemma unfolded not only in the realm of equations and scientific principles but also in the emotional landscape of their shared journey. The amulet, with its enigmatic energy, seemed to pulse with the gravity of the decisions that awaited them.

The world, captivated by the unfolding drama, awaited their response to the quantum dilemma. Would they embrace the scientific revelations at the cost of their privacy? Could the love they shared withstand the scrutiny and ethical quandaries that accompanied their extraordinary connection?

As Emily and David stood at this crossroads, their hearts entwined and their destinies interwoven with the threads of quantum entanglement, they faced a choice that would shape not only the trajectory of their love story but also the way humanity perceived the delicate dance between science and matters of the heart.

The quantum dilemma, a crucible of moral and emotional complexity, challenged the very essence of their connection. Emily and David would navigate the uncharted territories of ethics, love, and the delicate balance between scientific curiosity and the sanctity of their shared intimacy.

UNRAVELING THE MYSTERY

In the wake of the quantum dilemma, Emily and David found themselves on a journey of discovery—an exploration that transcended the boundaries of science, love, and the enigmatic forces that bound them together.

The laboratory, once a sanctuary of scientific inquiry, now became the epicenter of unraveling the mystery that surrounded the amulet and their quantum connection. David, fueled by a relentless curiosity, delved into experiments that sought to decode the intricacies of quantum entanglement without compromising the essence of their connection.

As the instruments hummed with precision and data unfolded like the pages of an intricate novel, David and his team ventured into the uncharted territories of the quantum realm. The amulet, suspended in a magnetic field of scientific scrutiny, pulsed with a rhythm that seemed to respond to the unfolding mysteries.

Emily, equally intrigued by the scientific exploration and the emotional resonance of their connection, stood by David's side. Together, they navigated the delicate balance between unveiling the secrets of the amulet and preserving the sanctity of their shared experiences.

Through late nights and fervent discussions, the laboratory became a crucible where scientific principles intertwined with the threads of their love story. As equations and hypotheses filled the air, Emily and David grappled with the complexities of tampering with the quantum unknown and the ethical responsibility that came with it.

The amulet, once a silent witness, now played an active role in the experiments. It became a focal point—a quantum anchor that held the key to understanding the entangled dance of particles and emotions. As the mysteries began to unfold, the laboratory echoed with the whispers of a connection that surpassed the boundaries of the known universe.

Yet, with each revelation, a sense of caution lingered. The quantum realm, unfathomable and unpredictable, carried the weight of uncertainty. The more they sought to unravel the mystery, the more questions emerged, challenging their understanding of the very forces that connected them.

With scientific exploration, Emily and David grappled with the consequences of their discoveries. The world, eager to comprehend the enigma of the amulet and the quantum connection, awaited their revelations. The laboratory, pulsating with the energy of both scientific inquiry and emotional vulnerability, became a stage where the cosmic and the personal converged.

In the journey of unraveling the mystery, Emily and David faced not only the challenges of quantum physics but also the complexities of the human heart. The amulet, a bridge between dimensions, held the promise of unveiling truths that transcended both science and love—an unfolding saga that would shape the destiny of their connection and the narratives of those who witnessed the dance between the quantum and the metaphysical.

THE INFINITE POSSIBILITIES

In the wake of scientific revelations and the delicate dance with the quantum unknown, Emily and David found themselves standing on the threshold of infinite possibilities. The amulet, once a mysterious artifact, now held the key to a realm where the boundaries of reality and imagination blurred.

As they continued their exploration, the laboratory became a crucible of experimentation and wonder. The amulet, suspended in a delicate balance of magnetic fields and quantum energies, pulsated with a rhythm that seemed to echo the very heartbeat of the cosmos.

Through their scientific endeavors, Emily and David discovered that the amulet was not just a conduit for their connection—it was a gateway to infinite dimensions. The quantum realm, unfurling before them like a cosmic tapestry, revealed pathways to alternate realities, parallel timelines, and the vastness of the multiverse.

In the laboratory's dim glow, equations danced on whiteboards, computers hummed with computational might, and the air buzzed with the excitement of untapped potential. The amulet, resonating with the energies of the quantum realm, became a beacon guiding them through the unexplored territories of existence.

As they delved deeper, the boundaries between science and metaphysics blurred. The infinite possibilities presented themselves not only in the form of scientific phenomena but also in the nuances of their love story. The letters, once carriers of thoughts and dreams, now held the power to traverse not just the spans of time but the vast expanses of alternate realities.

In their shared moments of revelation, Emily and David glimpsed the myriad paths their lives could have taken in different dimensions. They saw versions of themselves living different stories, making alternate choices, and existing in realms where the quantum connection unfolded in unique and unforeseen ways.

The amulet, a cosmic compass guiding them through the infinite possibilities of the multiverse, became a symbol of their intertwined destinies. Emily and David, standing at the nexus of quantum entanglement and love, began to fathom the depth of their connection—a connection that transcended the limitations of a single reality.

Yet, with the allure of infinite possibilities came a profound responsibility. The choices they made, both in the laboratory and the recesses of their hearts, rippled across the multiverse. The amulet, attuned to the quantum fabric of existence, resonated with the echoes of potential realities.

With exploration unfolding, Emily and David grappled with the weight of decisions that could alter the very course of their lives. The infinite possibilities, while tantalizing, carried the burden of consequence, challenging them to navigate the complexities of love, science, and the uncharted territories of the quantum realm.

In the glow of the laboratory's lights, the amulet continued to pulsate, a beacon amidst the cosmic vastness—a reminder that their connection, woven through the threads of time and space, held the potential to shape not only their destinies but the very fabric of the multiverse itself. The journey of infinite possibilities beckoned, and Emily and David stood poised to explore the boundless horizons that awaited them.

CONVERGENCE

In the culmination of their cosmic journey, Emily and David stood at the nexus of convergence—the point where the threads of science, love, and the quantum unknown intricately intertwined. The laboratory, once a realm of experimentation, now pulsated with the anticipation of a revelation that could reshape the very fabric of their existence.

The amulet, suspended in the center of a magnetic field, seemed to resonate with the culmination of their shared discoveries. The infinite possibilities they had glimpsed, the alternate realities they had explored, and the complexities of their connection converged into a singular moment, pregnant with potential.

As equations reached their apex and the quantum energies surged, Emily and David faced the threshold of a decision that would echo across the multiverse. The scientific community, the world at large, and the very forces that bound them together awaited the revelation born from the union of science and love.

In the quietude of the laboratory, where the hum of machines blended with the resonance of their hearts, Emily and David reached a shared understanding—an unspoken agreement that their connection, while enigmatic and ethereal, held a significance that transcended the boundaries of both quantum physics and human emotion.

With a steady hand and a shared gaze, they made a choice—a choice that acknowledged the potential of the quantum connection and the responsibilities it entailed. The amulet, responding to the energies of their decision, glowed with an otherworldly luminosity, casting a spectral light that seemed to bridge the gap between the tangible and the metaphysical.

In the moments that followed, the laboratory became a focal point for a convergence of energies. The amulet, now a conduit for the convergence of quantum forces, emitted a symphony of light and sound that echoed through the multiverse. The boundaries between realities blurred, and the infinite possibilities they had glimpsed coalesced into a singular narrative—a story written in the cosmic language of love and connection.

As the energies subsided, Emily and David felt a profound shift in the quantum currents. The amulet, once a mysterious artifact, now bore the imprints of their shared journey—an emblem of the convergence of science, love, and the infinite possibilities of the multiverse.

In the aftermath of this cosmic convergence, a sense of peace settled over Emily and David. The world, still captivated by their story, witnessed the transformative power of their connection. The laboratory, now hallowed ground where the quantum and the metaphysical had merged, became a symbol of the extraordinary tapestry woven by two souls connected across dimensions.

The journey, marked by love against the odds, ethical dilemmas, and the pursuit of scientific discovery, reached a point of convergence—a point where Emily and David, bound by the enigmatic amulet and the quantum forces that linked them, stood as architects of their shared destiny.

The amulet, now aglow with the echoes of their decisions, continued to pulse with the rhythm of the cosmos. Emily and David, their connection now a beacon of understanding that reached beyond the limits of the known universe, embraced the beauty of convergence—a beauty that celebrated the harmonious interplay of love, science, and the boundless possibilities that existed within the infinite expanse of the multiverse.

EPILOGUE: LOVE BEYOND DIMENSIONS

In the aftermath of cosmic convergence, Emily and David found themselves immersed in a reality that transcended the confines of conventional understanding. The amulet, once a catalyst for their quantum connection, now rested against their hearts as a symbol of a journey that had woven together the tapestry of love and science.

The world, having witnessed the extraordinary saga of Emily and David, embraced the legacy of their story. The laboratory, where scientific revelations and quantum mysteries had unfolded, became a sanctuary of inspiration for those who dared to explore the interplay between the tangible and the metaphysical.

Emily and David, now celebrated as pioneers of a love that defied dimensions, continued to navigate the nuances of their connection. The letters, timeless and imbued with the echoes of shared experiences, served as a testament to the enduring nature of a bond that reached beyond the constraints of time and space.

As the years unfolded, the legacy of their story expanded beyond the borders of scientific journals and academic discourse. The amulet, with its enigmatic energy, became a symbol of hope for those who believed in the possibility of love that extended beyond the known dimensions of existence.

In the quiet moments of reflection, Emily and David marveled at the impact of their shared journey. The quantum connection, once a source of mystery and intrigue, had become a beacon for others seeking to unravel the complexities of love, connection, and the boundless frontiers of the human heart.

Their love story, written in the cosmic language of the multiverse, echoed through the ages—a narrative that celebrated the convergence of science and emotion, the beauty of ethical choices, and the infinite possibilities that lay within the quantum unknown.

The amulet, now a cherished relic, continued to radiate a gentle glow—a reminder that love, in its purest form, held the power to transcend dimensions. Emily and David, intertwined by the threads of destiny and the enigmatic forces that had brought them together, reveled in the beauty of a connection that echoed beyond the known boundaries of the universe.

As they stood on the precipice of a future shaped by love beyond dimensions, Emily and David embraced the enduring truth—they were not merely participants in a cosmic dance but architects of a love story that resonated across the vast expanse of the multiverse.

And so, the echoes of their love reverberated through the quantum currents, a timeless melody that celebrated the extraordinary journey of two souls who dared to explore the limitless possibilities of love beyond the dimensions of time and space.

www.ingramcontent.com/pod-product-compliance
Lightning Source LLC
LaVergne TN
LVHW012047070526
838201LV00082B/3849